W9-BBB-437

For Amelia

First U.S. edition 1995

Library of Congress Cataloging-in-Publication Data

West, Colin.
One day in the jungle / Colin West. — 1st U.S. ed.
Summary: Starting with a butterfly, each successive animal sneezes
louder until the elephant blows away the jungle.
ISBN 1-56402-646-9
[1. Jungle animals — Fiction.   2. Sneeze — Fiction.]   I. Title.
PZ7.W517440n   1995
[E] — dc20   95-7888

2 4 6 8 10 9 7 5 3 1

Printed in Hong Kong

The pictures in this book were done in pencil and watercolor.

Candlewick Press
2067 Massachusetts Avenue
Cambridge, Massachusetts 02140

One Day in the Jungle

COLIN WEST

CANDLEWICK PRESS
CAMBRIDGE, MASSACHUSETTS

One day in the jungle
there was a little sneeze.

"Bless you, Butterfly!"
said Lizard.

Next day in the jungle
there was a not-quite-so-little sneeze.

"Bless you, Lizard!" said Parrot.

Next day in the jungle
there was a medium-sized sneeze.

"Bless you, Parrot!" said Monkey.

Next day in the jungle
there was a big sneeze.

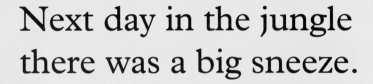

"Bless you, Monkey!" said Tiger.

Next day in the jungle
there was a very big sneeze.

"Bless you, Tiger!"
said Hippo.

Next day in the jungle
there was an enormous sneeze.

"Bless you, Hippo!"
said Elephant.

Next day in the jungle
there was a **GIGANTIC** sneeze.

"Bless me!" said Elephant.
"I've blown away the jungle!"